MAGIC IN THE OUTFIELD

#1

MAGIC IN THE OUTFIELD

LOREN LONG & PHIL BILDNER

ALADDIN PAPERBACKS
NEW YORK   LONDON   TORONTO   SYDNEY

ALADDIN PAPERBACKS
An imprint of Simon & Schuster Children's Publishing Division
1230 Avenue of the Americas, New York, NY 10020
Text copyright © 2007 by Phil Bildner and Loren Long
Illustrations copyright © 2007 by Loren Long
All rights reserved, including the right of reproduction
in whole or in part in any form.
ALADDIN PAPERBACKS and related logo are registered trademarks of
Simon & Schuster, Inc.
Originally published in 2007 as *Barnstormers: Game 1* by Simon &
Schuster Books for Young Readers.
The text of this book was set in Century 731 BT.
Manufactured in the United States of America
First Aladdin Paperbacks edition February 2009
4 6 8 10 9 7 5
Library of Congress Cataloging-in-Publication Data
Long, Loren.
[Game 1]
Magic in the outfield / by Loren Long and Phil Bildner.—1st Aladdin
Paperbacks ed.
p. cm.—(Sluggers ; 1)
Originally published in 2007 under title: Game 1.
Summary: In the late 1800s, a baseball with strange powers belonging to
their late father works wonders for three children and a traveling baseball
team which must raise $10,000.
ISBN-13: 978-1-4169-1884-4 (pbk)
ISBN-10: 1-4169-1884-1 (pbk)
[1. Baseball—Fiction. 2. Brothers and sisters—Fiction. 3. Supernatural—
Fiction. 4. Cincinnati (Ohio)—History—19th century—Fiction.]
I. Bildner, Phil. II. Title.
PZ7.L8555Mag 2009
[Fic]—dc22
2008028973
0411 OFF

To Bart Giamatti,
Hank Aaron,
Vin Scully,
Cal Ripken Jr.,
Peter Gammons,
and all the other
believers in baseball
and keepers of the game.
—P. B.

To my father,
William G. Long,
who introduced me
to the Big Red Machine.
I'd still rather go to a ball game
with you than anyone.
—L. L.

Contents

THE BALLAD OF THE BALL

An early February morn
All bright and cold and clear,
Is where this well-worn tale was born,
So gather close and hear—
Yes, train your ears and hear.

★

The month was only six days old,
When son and father stepped
Into their yard to toss a ball
The second son? He slept—
A babe beside them. Slept.

★

Far up above this game of catch
An eagle circled nigh,
Then swooped, a flash of feathers, down
To bear that babe on high—
That bundled babe on high!

Woe and panic! Worry! Grief!
A father's desperate scour
From evening through the dark of night,
Hour after hour,
Fruitless hour after hour.

★

Anon! The sun arose anew.
And misery descended
On a father, bound for home,
Down-hearted, empty-handed—
Distraught and empty-handed.

★

His wife, his elder son, and yes
His little daughter too,
clung to father and to hope,
And prayed for what to do.
What's a broken family to do?

As the hours tumbled on
And day returned to night,
Mother, son, and daughter slept.
The father studied their plight—
Their sad and hopeless plight.

★

A sudden noise! Right then! A knock!
What news? What grief or bliss?
Then at the door a beggar stood asking
"Do you seek this—
This babe, do you seek this?"

★

Taking babe into his arms
The father met two eyes:
One cloudy as a stormy day,
And one a clear bright blue sky—
A brilliant springtime sky.

And as the thankful father stared
In shaken disbelief,
The dirty, tattered old man spoke
Of sorrow, pain, and grief—
Looming like a thief.

★

So please teach your children well
To stay close when they roam,
And closely watch what others don't,
For that's the beacon home—
The brightest beacon home.

★

The beggar then withdrew a ball
From within his dirty sleeve,
Tossed it up, then watched it fall.
"With this you will believe.
Hold this and you'll believe."

As the father held the ball
He thought he felt it quiver,
And seeing how it fit his palm,
Felt what it could deliver,
What magic it would deliver.

★

Amazed the father stood and watched
The old man turn and go.
An eagle's cry then filled the sky,
Softened by falling snow—
Rare and wonderful falling snow.

★

And when the old man disappeared,
The father stood and cried,
Then took his miracle, blessed babe
To his family inside—
His mended family inside.

PROLOGUE

★

July, 1899, Washington, D.C.

hy were you fighting with Mom?" Ruby asked Uncle Owen as he wheeled his chair down the stone path that led from his back porch to the wooden table in the middle of the yard.

Griffith helped align the chair and peered sharply at his uncle's face, waiting for him to answer his younger sister.

"We weren't . . . we weren't fighting," Uncle Owen stammered, absentmindedly rubbing the stump of his leg. "There were just some . . . Listen, I need to talk to you about some things, and we don't have much time."

Uncle Owen lifted the cloth from his lap, dipped it in the basin of water hooked to the armrest of his wheelchair, and dabbed his brow.

"There are some things you must know," he continued. He faced Ruby and Griffith, seated side by side on the bench connected to the table. "And they must remain among us. No one else can know. No one."

"You hear that, Grammy?" Griffith nudged his brother, who was sitting on the table.

"You hear that, Griff?" Graham mocked.

Ruby smiled and playfully patted Graham's swinging leg. Their little brother always seemed to make her smile. Even at times like this.

She reached over and wiped his tear-stained cheeks. Whenever she had cried

today—and her tears had flowed steadily—
Graham had cried too, harder and louder.

Only Griffith hadn't cried. Not once the
entire day. It had made Ruby angry. How
could you not cry at your own father's
funeral?

She flipped her hair off the back of her
neck. The heat and humidity were unbear-
able. It had been like this all day—during the
service at the church, during the procession
to the cemetery, and then at the burial.

The storm afterward had provided no relief. But what a storm it had been: relentless, torrential sheets; streaked lightning igniting a charcoal sky; and ground-shaking thunderclaps. All that remained now from the storm were the fading flashes that still lit the trees and the leftover rumbles that growled in the distance.

"Uncle Owen, mind if I ask you a question?" Ruby said.

"Sure thing," Uncle Owen replied, "but make it quick. Your mother will be coming to get you shortly."

"Mother said we're going to be barnstormers. What does that mean?"

"I'll tell you." Uncle Owen reached up to ruffle Graham's hair just like their father always did. "Barnstorming is when folks travel around the country presenting plays, giving lectures, or performing exhibitions like dancing, tightrope walking, or baseball."

"Baseball?" Graham asked.

"That's right, partner, baseball. It can be lucrative. Very lucrative. Do you know what that means?"

"It means you can make a lot of money," Ruby answered first.

"You sure can. That's why a few of the Rough Riders from the war have formed the Travelin' Nine. They're barnstorming to raise money for your mother. A great deal of money." Uncle Owen glanced back at the house, and then he drew them in closer, looking them each in the eye. "Your mother needs you. More than you can imagine. More than *she* can imagine." He let out a short breath. "Now I have something for you. Wait here."

He wheeled his chair across the yard to his garden. From around his neck and underneath his shirt, he lifted out a set of keys and leaned down to a large trunk that rested on the ground next to a picket fence.

He unlocked each of the three locks, first the middle one, then the two sides. Using both hands and most of his strength, he lifted the lid. He peered inside and carefully removed a small metal box. He shut the lid and fastened the locks in the reverse order, first the sides, followed by the middle.

Uncle Owen rolled back through the puddles that dotted the yard, easing to a gentle stop in front of his niece and nephews.

"Your father wanted you to have this," Uncle Owen said, speaking to the box resting in his lap. "But remember, you mustn't tell a soul. No one can know."

Slowly, Uncle Owen unhooked the clasps, removed the cover, and reached inside for an item wrapped in burlap. He placed the bundle in his lap and set the metal box on the ground. Then, gently, he peeled back the burlap and lifted out a round object.

Graham's eyes lit up. "Is that my baseball?"

Uncle Owen nodded once.

"What happened to it?"

"War." Uncle Owen looked them each in the eye again and then back at the object resting in his cupped hand. He leaned forward and as he did, Griffith took the ball from his hands.

The moment he touched the ball, Griffith felt a chill pass through him. He shuddered. He ran a finger over the stitching, teased a loose thread, and slid a fingernail into the nicks. Then he caressed the rawhide. It reminded him of his father's calloused hand. In a way, it almost felt as if he were holding his father's hand. Then he raised the ball to his face and peered into the hole.

"What happened here?" he asked.

Uncle Owen didn't answer.

Griffith shook the ball gently. Whatever

had caused the hole was probably still embedded within.

He passed the ball to Ruby.

She held it in her open hand like she would hold a small animal. Like Griffith, she was drawn to the acorn-size hole. She inserted her pinky, but when she tried to move it around, it was too snug a fit.

She handed the ball to Graham.

Just like Griffith had, Graham teased the stitching and slid a nail into the nicks. Then he lifted the ball to his eye and looked into the hole before gently shaking the sphere.

Graham brushed his tear-stained cheek with a shoulder sleeve and stared at *his* baseball in *his* hand. The last time Graham had held the ball was when he had given it to his father as he boarded the train to San Antonio. When he was leaving for the war. For some reason Graham had been convinced that the baseball—which for as long as he could recall had sat safely encased atop the end table beside his bed—needed to go with his father. Maybe he had been right. Unlike Uncle Owen, Graham's father had survived the war whole only to die near home in a mysterious boating accident.

Graham leaned in and placed the ball back in Uncle Owen's hand. At the very moment he did, the creaky patio screen door swung open and out stepped their mother.

"I'm sorry, kids," she said as she hurried down the pathway. "Time to go. Uncle Owen's kind neighbor has offered us a ride to the depot. If we leave now, we can make the earlier train."

"Elizabeth, I need a few more minutes with them." Uncle Owen tucked the baseball under his leg. "I need—"

"No," Elizabeth interrupted flatly. "We must catch that train."

9

"Mom, please," Griffith pleaded. He hated hearing the edge in her voice. "Uncle Owen's telling us—"

"Griff, this is not for discussion. Whatever it is, it will have to wait. Say your good-byes."

Griffith said no more. The last thing he wanted was to cause his mother any additional grief.

"Elizabeth," Uncle Owen said in a softened tone. He pivoted his chair and faced his sister-in-law directly. "I must talk to Griff. You know—"

"Owen, I said it will have to wait."

"I'm not sure it can." The beads of sweat on his brow had grown to the size of bullets.

"I don't care!" Elizabeth snapped. "I've had enough for one day. I've had enough for a lifetime. The things you told me . . . on top of everything else . . ." Her words trailed off.

"Two minutes," Uncle Owen said as calmly as he could. "Please, Elizabeth. That's all I'm asking for."

She glared at her husband's brother and then let out a deep sigh. "Two minutes." She lifted Graham off the table. "But say good-bye to the others before you do."

"Thank you." Uncle Owen bowed his head.

Ruby went first.

"I love you," she whispered in her uncle's ear as she bent over and hugged him. His body felt so bony and frail.

"Be together. Always."

"I love you, too, Ruby," he said, slipping the ball back into her hand. "Be together. Always."

Ruby nodded. She squeezed the baseball and slid it into her pocket.

Graham went next.

"I'll miss you, Uncle O."

As the tears streamed down his face, he took his uncle's cloth, dipped it into the basin, and dabbed the red and raised scars that crisscrossed his uncle's neck.

"I'll miss you too, partner." Uncle Owen ruffled his youngest nephew's hair one final time.

Griffith waited until Ruby and Graham were back in the house before stepping closer to his uncle. Just like he had been the last to say good-bye to his father at the cemetery, he would be the last to bid farewell now.

"Take care of your family." Uncle Owen placed his hand on Griffith's shoulder, like

Griffith's father used to, like Griffith's father had done only *days* before. "They need you. Be strong."

Griffith nodded.

Uncle Owen lifted his hand and placed it on Griffith's cheek. "Griff, great danger lies ahead."

"What kind of danger?" Griffith's eyes met his uncle's.

"An unspeakable kind." Uncle Owen choked on his words. "I will tell you. I will write to you and explain. For now, try not to be afraid. Watch and listen. Things will speak to you. In different ways."

"I don't understand," Griffith said.

"But you will," Uncle Owen's voice broke, and for the first time, instead of dabbing his brow with the cloth, he patted his eyes. "Griff, see the things that others don't."

1

★

The Piggy Town Showdown
ONE MONTH LATER IN CINCINNATI

raham had fire in his eyes. He stood toe-to-toe with the older boy, and no matter how hard Ruby tugged at him, he pulled away, refusing to back down.

"You think you can beat the Travelin' Nine?" Graham pointed at the boy's chest. "You don't know what you're talking about."

The older boy waved the flyer back in Graham's face. "You don't know what *you're* talkin' 'bout, *pip-squeak!*"

Graham clenched his fists. "The Travelin'

Nine can beat any team from your piggy town!"

"Piggy town?" The boy laughed. "Try Porkopolis, small fry. That's what we in Cincinnati call our city. Porkopolis: the pork-packin' capital of the world."

"Piggy town!" Graham repeated, louder. "No piggy-town team can beat the Travelin' Nine."

Ruby grabbed at her little brother again, afraid that he would try to tackle the other boy right into the Ohio River.

BALLISTS: *players.*

"Let me tell you somethin' else." The older boy towered over Graham. "When it comes to baseball, we were first. We had the first pro team in the whole country. We here in Cincinnati take our baseball very seriously."

"So! Who cares?" Graham fired back.

"Listen, runt. You really think a team of Cincinnati ballists is gonna lose to some travelin'-sideshow band of barnstormers?"

That was the final straw. Graham lunged at the older boy and shoved him in the gut. The older boy winced and doubled over, but only for a brief moment, and for not nearly as long as Graham had hoped.

"Is that the best you can do, shrimp?" The older boy stood up, taller than ever. He pushed Graham away. Graham stumbled but somehow managed to remain on his feet.

"Now you've done it!" Graham shouted. He lowered his head, drew back both fists, and charged. And as Graham leaped at his nemesis, from out of nowhere he was plucked from the air.

"Whoa!" Griffith said. "Easy, Grambo!"

"You're gonna be sorry!" the older boy said even as he backed off and away. "Sorry you ever came to Cincinnati!"

Graham struggled to escape Griffith's grasp, but years of wrestling with his big brother had taught him there was no use.

Roebling Suspension bridge

He stopped flailing his arms and slowly unclenched his fists.

"Grammy, you can't do that." Griffith loosened his grip.

"He started it."

"It doesn't matter. We're new here. You can't go around picking fights."

"Why not?" Ruby flashed an amused smile at her older brother and pointed. "It worked."

In the distance they could see the boy pausing on the Roebling Suspension Bridge; he seemed to be reading the Travelin' Nine flyer. Then he quickly stuffed it into his back pocket before heading off.

"He started it," Graham repeated, crossing his arms over his chest.

Griffith sighed. He knew better than to continue arguing with his brother. Besides, they all had something more important to do. They had to promote the ball game. They

had to help distribute the flyers that both Professor Lance and Bubbles were lugging in their overstuffed satchels farther up the road.

Griffith reached into his pocket and pulled out one of the flyers. He thought about his mother's words from earlier that day.

"We need people at the game, Griff," she had said when she pulled him aside. In her eyes he thought he saw something he'd seen once before, but it was so long ago he no longer knew if it was real or just a dream. "Lots of people."

The barnstormers were trying to raise money. A lot of money. Thousands of dollars. Ten thousand dollars. Griffith knew it. Ruby and Graham knew it too.

"What is it?" Ruby said.

"What is what?" Griffith replied, folding the advertisement back up.

"You know what I'm talking about, Griff. There's something you're not telling me."

"Ruby, how many times do I have to say it? I'm not keeping anything from you."

"I know Uncle Owen told you something the night of Daddy's funeral. I know he did, but I don't understand why you won't tell me."

Griffith looked sadly at his sister. He took a breath as if to speak, hesitated, and shook his head. What good would it do, he thought, for Ruby to worry more than she already did? He knew that both Ruby and Graham wanted to know, needed to know, deserved to know what Uncle Owen had told him that night in his yard when he gave Guy's children his old baseball. But Griffith still wasn't sure he knew how to explain the curious caution their uncle had issued.

Griffith sighed. "Come on. We need to catch up to Bubbles and the Professor. We have work to do."

TRUE AMERICAN HEROES
TRUE AMERICAN SPORTSMEN

THE BRAVE SOLDIERS FROM SAN JUAN HILL
THE VALIANT VETERANS OF THE SPANISH-AMERICAN WAR

ROOSEVELT'S ROUGH RIDERS **VS.** THE QUEEN CITY'S FINEST, THE CINCINNATI SWINE

☞ RAIN OR SHINE ☜

MONDAY AUGUST [7] 1899 HIGH NOON

AFFORDABLE ADMISSION

AMERICA'S

New

NATIONAL PASTIME ON DISPLAY

An Afternoon of Athleticism, Artistry, & Americana

2

★

Spreading the Word

orget that boy by the bridge," Bubbles declared. "I don't want any of you to get the wrong impression about *my* city." He leaped into the middle of Vine Street. "Welcome to Cincinnati! The Queen City of the West!" He dropped his satchel and spun like a top until he fell to the pavement. Griffith, Ruby, and Graham laughed.

Bubbles was quite the chatterbox, and even though Professor Lance had made it perfectly clear that Bubbles's primary purpose would be to make sure they didn't get lost, it didn't appear as though Bubbles had heard Professor Lance at all (and not just because Bubbles was missing part of an ear).

"Cincinnati is *bubbling* with history," Bubbles said, struggling to stand. "Right now we're in Hamilton County, named for Alexander Hamilton, one of this country's founding fathers. And speaking of great Americans, did you know I'm related to the president of the United States?"

"You're related to President McKinley?" Ruby eyed him sideways. She knew Bubbles was prone to stretching the truth.

"Oh, no, not the current president." Bubbles cleared his throat. "I'm talking about the great state of Ohio's own Rutherford B. Hayes, nineteenth president of the U. S. of A. Old Rutherford's my third cousin's aunt's brother's nephew."

"Is that so?" Ruby asked.

"I think so," Bubbles replied. He scratched

at what remained of his left ear. "Well, let's just say it's possible."

By the time they made it up Elm Street and across to Findlay Market, everyone had heard more than enough out of Bubbles.

Fortunately, Findlay Market was abuzz. It teemed with a carnival-like excitement. Vendors galore lined Elder Street selling poultry, flowers, produce, fresh fish—anything and everything! Throngs of people reveled in the sights, sounds, and smells.

This was the perfect place to spread the word of the Travelin' Nine. So with far too many flyers still needing to be distributed, Professor Lance sent the children off on their own to do their duty.

Both Griffith and Ruby took polite approaches, but neither had much luck. Most people passed them by without so much as a glance. But Graham was a different story. He challenged anyone and everyone who

crossed his path, an approach that worked
like a charm.

"Want to see the Cincinnati Swine get beat
by a bunch of out-of-towners?" he goaded.

An approach that worked like a charm

"How badly do you think the Cincinnati Swine will lose to the Travelin' Nine?" he teased.

At the very least, people were amused and took a flyer. At the very worst, people were annoyed, but they took a flyer anyway.

"There's one last Cincinnati sight we need to see," Professor Lance said after all the flyers were finally gone. He adjusted the cord of the patch that covered his left eye.

Professor Lance steered the group onto a trolley car, and through the streets of Cincinnati they went. As Professor Lance talked about the history of his home state, Griffith found himself gazing at Ruby's pocket—the one in which she'd carefully tucked away the baseball. He forced his eyes to look out the window, but his mind turned, yet again, to the cryptic warning Uncle Owen had given him about the ball. What could Uncle Owen's prediction of danger mean?

Danger? Playing baseball? No matter how many times Griffith chewed over their unfinished conversation, he couldn't make sense of it. Nor could he rid himself of the chilling fear in his stomach every time he thought about his family. How he wished he'd had just a few more minutes with Uncle Owen to hear the whole story. Nothing, he thought grimly, could be worse than this uncertainty that gnawed at him and made him keep secrets from his brother and sister.

Before they knew it, they had arrived at their destination: League Park.

"Why can't we play here?" Ruby asked as soon as she saw the enormous grandstand and manicured field.

"This is where the Red Stockings play," Professor Lance replied.

"Why can't we play here?" she asked again.

"Maybe someday," Professor Lance said.

"The Red Stockings are a professional team. We're just barnstormers. As good as we may be, we're no match for them."

"That's not true!" Graham declared. "The Travelin' Nine can beat any team."

Professor Lance turned to Ruby, shrugged, and smiled. "Your father would have insisted I take you here," he said, his hand resting on Graham's shoulder. "In his mind, no trip to Cincinnati would be complete without a visit to this cathedral of baseball."

Ruby slid her hand into her side pocket. The baseball was still there. Of course it was still there. Just like it was *always* going to be there. She ran her fingertips over the seams and stuck her pinky into the odd, acorn-size hole.

Then, for a moment, she felt the baseball tremble. Or at least she thought it did. But it couldn't have.

Could it?

"Why can't we play here?"

3

★

Game Day!

ime to hit the field!" Graham clapped and pointed to the Travelin' Nine's pregame practice. Griffith didn't respond.

"I need to take my cut," Graham said, pretending to swing a bat. "Need to loosen up my cannon." He pretended to throw a pitch.

Griffith didn't answer. He was so lost in thought, he didn't even hear his younger brother.

He ran his hand through his thick hair as he gazed out toward the trees beyond left garden. With the Travelin' Nine's first match

CUT:
a swing.

CANNON:
a strong throwing arm.

MATCH:
a game.

almost set to begin, all he could think about were the words Uncle Owen had said to him on the night of the funeral. Griffith still had so many questions, and too few answers.

"Come on, Grammy." Ruby tapped her younger brother on the shoulder and glanced at Griffith. "I'll head down with you."

Graham grabbed his sister by the hand and pulled her toward the field.

"Slow down!" Ruby tugged. "I need to ask you something."

"But the Travelin' Nine are waiting for me," Graham replied.

"I know they are," Ruby answered.

Ruby was aware the Travelin' Nine wanted Graham on the field almost as much as Graham wanted to be on the field. Baseball players are a most superstitious breed, and her younger brother had become the Travelin' Nine's good luck charm. At every practice Graham always took one swing, and afterward, the Travelin' Nine always seemed to smack the ball harder, throw the ball faster, and field the ball more cleanly.

"Do you think Griff is keeping something from us?" Ruby asked.

"Like what?" Graham asked back.

"I think there's something he's not telling us."

Graham stared blankly at his sister.

Ruby sighed. "You have no idea what I'm talking about, do you?"

"Ruby, all I know—"

"Let's go, Grammy!" Doc Linden suddenly shouted from the field. "We're waiting for you!"

"And we haven't got all afternoon!" Happy added. "We've got a game to play!"

With that, Graham charged onto the field.

4

★

Graham Takes His Cut

STRIKER'S BOX:
area in which the
striker (now known
as the batter) stood
when it was his
turn to hit. Also
known as the
"striker's line."

DISH:
home plate.

LUMBER:
baseball bat. Also
called "timber."

HURLER:
pitcher.

itting on the players' bench, Ruby couldn't help but smile when Graham stepped into the striker's box.

At the plate, Graham pounded the dish three times, just like Bubbles did whenever he was up, and he wagged his lumber high over his head the way Scribe did each time he stared down a hurler. Then he shuffled his feet into a wider stance, just like Woody did whenever he got ready to swing, and he flapped his elbow four times the way Tales did each time he dug in.

"You're only getting one!" Happy called

from the pitcher's line. "Make it count."

"You watching, Ruby?" Graham asked without taking his eyes from Happy.

"You know I am," Ruby answered. She stood up and stepped forward for a closer look.

Graham peeked back to the Travelin' Nine's backstop. "You watching, Ma . . . I mean, Guy?"

Ruby held her breath.

Guy wasn't really Guy. Guy was their mother, Elizabeth. Elizabeth played catcher for the Travelin' Nine. That had been their father's position, and he had played the position like few others had ever played it before. But he was no longer here, so if their mother didn't fill in at backstop, the Travelin' Nine couldn't field a club.

Ruby now stood alongside Griffith, who had finally joined them down at the field. She glanced over at him.

Ruby and Griffith both understood that their mother wasn't *allowed* to play baseball. Not as a woman, at least. So on the field everyone

PITCHER'S LINE: *marker where the pitcher begins his pitch. Now known as the pitching rubber.*

BACKSTOP: *catcher. Also called "behind" (see page 111).*

41

Graham stepped into the striker's box.

called her Guy, and she wore a two-sizes-too-large Travelin' Nine uniform and a cap pulled way down to hide the darkest brown eyes on either side of the Mississippi or Mason-Dixon.

On the field, Elizabeth *was* Guy.

"You know I'm watching, Grammy," Guy said, holding up a target for the pitch. "Give it a ride!"

Crack!

PILL: *baseball. Also called the "rock" (see page 70).*

What a ride he gave it! On one bounce, the pill hopped into the line of trees beyond right garden. And even though it was only batting practice, Graham still raced full speed around the bases and slid into home plate.

"Safe!" he signaled while lying on his back.

Ruby applauded her brother and then looked back to her mother pounding her mitt and lowering her mask. Ruby smiled. It didn't hurt that their mother had the softest hands on the team and that she could throw the pill harder than anyone, except maybe Woody.

Things would be fine . . . just as long as she was never found out.

5

★

Warming Up

ow that he had taken his cut and the fans were filing in, Graham sat down on the players' bench and watched the Travelin' Nine get down to business.

At home plate, Guy handed the ball to Happy, who then flipped it to Doc. Doc pointed his timber out toward left garden, tossed the baseball into the air, and drew back his bat.

Whack!

Like a rocketed flare, the ball blasted off his bat, soaring high and long into the hazy summer sky. In an instant Crazy Feet

kicked the grass and gave chase. Way deep in left field, where the carpet of green sloped upward to a terrace and greeted the thick line of trees, he reached out his glove. The ball landed in his leather with a gentle pop.

"My friend," Doc said, turning to Happy, "life offers us very little in the way of sure things, but let me tell you, that there is one sure thing. Sky balls to left will land in Crazy Feet's glove. Guaranteed."

"Without a doubt," Happy replied. "Left field's the graveyard where fly balls go to die."

LEATHER:
baseball glove or mitt.

SKY BALL:
fly ball to the outfield or outer garden. Also sometimes referred to as a "cloud hunter" or a "rainmaker."

Graham gasped and covered his mouth. He couldn't believe what Happy had just said.

Neither could Happy, for that matter, and he flinched the moment the words left his lips. He turned around to his backstop.

"I'm so sorry," Happy whispered.

"It's okay." Guy managed a smile.

The last thing any of them wanted to hear was anything having to do with death and dying. Graham could see how much his mother missed his father every time she looked at him.

"It's okay, Happy." She squeezed a baseball into his rugged hand. "Honest, it's okay."

"He would have loved this." Happy faced the field again and flipped the ball to Doc. "A perfect summer day for the perfect summer game. I know he's smiling down on us."

"Guaranteed." Doc smiled as he hit a daisy cutter to the infielders.

DAISY CUTTER: ground ball. Also known as "grass clipper" (see page 68) or "ant killer" (see page 73).

48

"He would have loved this."

"*That's* a sure thing." Happy chuckled. "No doubt he's holding court in heaven as we speak."

"Pointing out the bald spots, one by one, where the position players stand!"

"Telling all the angels how the base paths have been worn down to the dirt like over-used rugs."

"Talking their angel ears off!"

"And with the way Guy talks baseball," Doc said, leaning on his lumber, "you know every last angel is listening to every last word. Guaranteed."

"Thanks, Doc." Her smile was no longer forced. "Thanks, Happy." She pounded her mitt like a baker pounds dough.

Graham was beaming as he raced back onto the field after practice. He joined the barnstormers gathered around home plate. "Look at this crowd," he said.

Indeed, the cranks were everywhere. They had completely filled the hillsides behind first base, and on the third base line they were already lined two and three deep along the entire length of the white picket fence that extended all the way into the outfield.

"From what I hear," Happy said to Graham, "we have you to thank for all these fans."

"From what I hear, you didn't take no for an answer," Doc agreed. "A natural. One heckuva seven-year-old salesman."

"You sure know how to close a deal."

"You could sell ice to an Eskimo!"

"Feathers to a bird!"

Both men laughed. Then at the same time they added, "Just like your dad."

CRANKS:
fans, usually the hometown fans. Also called "rooters" (see page 64).

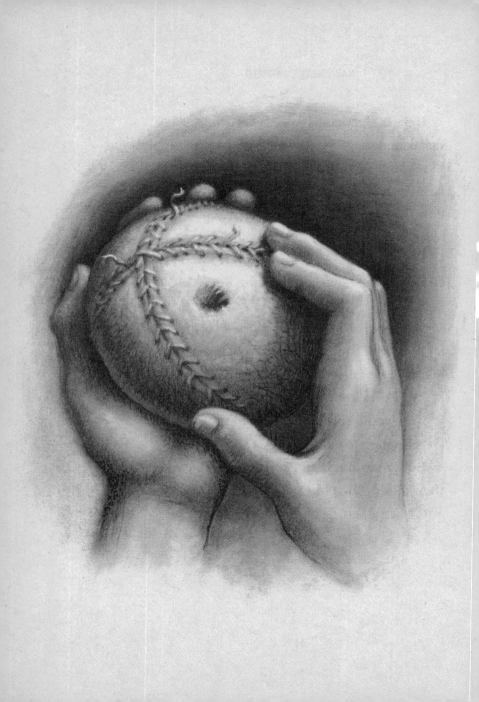

6

★

The Baseball

riffith cradled the baseball in the palm of his hand and slowly ran his finger over its loosened stitching. The ball was worn and tattered, and Griffith wondered what still held it together. One thing was certain, it didn't look like the balls the players were about to use down on the field.

During the war, Griffith's father had carried this baseball with him wherever he went. Cupping it now made Griffith feel somehow closer to his father, even though his dad was beyond reach.

Standing beneath the great oak on the hill beyond the right garden foul line, Griffith held the baseball low so that the players couldn't see it. Only his brother and sister next to him could. The baseball was theirs and theirs alone. No one else needed to know they had it.

Ruby was wiping her brow. There wasn't a breeze to be found on this August afternoon.

She stole a look over her shoulder. Professor Lance was playing first base, Tales was readying at second sack, and Woody was standing in right garden—none of the players had the least idea what the children were up to. She looked back at her older brother. He smiled, and when he did, Ruby noticed a touch of something in his face. She couldn't say for sure what it was, but she had been seeing that look more and more lately.

She placed her hand gently on top of the

RIGHT GARDEN:
right field. The outfield was once known as the garden. So left field was referred to as "left garden" and center field was called "center garden."

SACK:
base, or bag, as in "first sack" or "third bag."

ball. Her fingers wove into her brother's, and she slid her pinky over the odd, acorn-size hole that had tunneled a path nearly all the way through.

Graham soon placed his hand over his brother's and sister's.

"Like this?" he asked.

"Make sure your fingertips are on the ball," Griffith instructed.

They had held the ball like this, all three together, a few times. They hadn't planned to do so now, but it suddenly seemed right to all three of them.

"Dad should be here," Ruby said.

Griffith and Graham nodded.

"I miss him bad now that the game is about to start," Graham said softly.

"He was a great player," Ruby said, "and no one loved this moment before the game begins more than Dad."

"I . . . I can almost feel him nearby when I hold his old baseball," Graham murmured.

"It . . . well, it helps me feel like we're still a whole family even though he's no longer with us." Ruby and Graham looked solemnly at their older brother, taking comfort in his voice. The three Payne children stood silently, their hands on the ball and their

Watch and wait.

fingers intertwined with each other, looking down at the Travelin' Nine. A shudder ran through Griffith.

"Now what?" Graham asked in a voice barely above a whisper.

"Now," Ruby answered, "now I guess we watch and wait."

7

★

Play Ball!

own the right field
line, beneath the great
oak on the knoll in foul
territory, Griffith, Ruby, and Graham stood
with their eyes glued to the field, their hands
on their baseball.

On the diamond, the umpire—dressed in
a top hat, bow tie, and tuxedo tails—called
both captains together. Prancing and parad-
ing like a circus ringmaster, he announced
the ground rules in a booming voice.

"If any animal, bird, creature, or object
interferes with a batted ball in fair territory,"

The rooters gathered close to the field. . . .

the umpire concluded, "it's an automatic two-base hit. An automatic double."

Griffith looked around. Rooters gathered close to the field, and more cranks stood behind them, stretching on their tiptoes to see the game. A few fearless others sat perched atop the roof of the schoolhouse behind the picket fence in left.

ROOTERS: *fans; people who cheer at ball games. Also called "cranks" (see page 51).*

Griffith looked back at the field as the umpire prepared for the pregame coin flip. Usually a foot race between the two speediest players from each nine determined which team batted first, but both teams had agreed to the coin flip because of the heat.

"Heads," Graham whispered at exactly the same moment that Happy called, "Heads!"

"Heads it is!" the umpire declared.

"We'll take the field," Happy informed him.

The umpire pointed the Travelin' Nine to the field, then motioned to the Cincinnati Swine to prepare to bat.

"Striker to the line!"

"Striker to the line!" the umpire bellowed. He waved his top hat to the crowd and bowed like a conductor in front of his orchestra.

As Griffith watched the Travelin' Nine take their positions, all of the unanswered questions he had been living with since the night of his father's funeral reentered his head. And all of the secrets, too.

"STRIKER TO THE LINE!": what the umpire announced at the start of each contest. It was also called out at each batter's turn. Today the umpire yells, "Batter up!"

Griffith wasn't used to keeping secrets from Ruby and Graham, and from the way Ruby had been eyeing him and from the questions she'd been asking, he knew he wasn't very good at it either.

"Striker to the line!"

8

★

Top of the First

ere we go." **Griffith** bit his lower lip.

"C'mon, Happy!" Ruby cheered nervously.

Happy was always telling the Payne children that he had an unfair advantage when it came to pitching. "See here," he'd say, chuckling and holding up his hurling hand, "this here missing finger? Best thing that ever happened to me . . . makes the ball groove into the plate when I throw. Can't no one EVER tell all the time what a ball that comes from MY hand is gonna do

as it gets close to the striker." Griffith, Ruby, and Graham didn't know if it was the missing digit; or something else, like raw talent; or just good luck at the right time; but they knew that Happy was the lynchpin of the Travelin' Nine, and that without his masterful pitching and control of the field from the mound, they wouldn't be as strong a team.

Cincinnati's first batter stepped up to home plate. He nodded politely to the umpire and to Guy. Then, on Happy's first pitch, he smoked a grass clipper down to Doc at third.

"Leggit! Leggit!" chanted the rooters.

However, much to the home team's dismay, Doc's frozen rope across the infield retired the batter by a step.

One hand down.

The second Cincinnati batter came up to the plate. He nodded to the umpire and to Guy. Then, on Happy's second pitch, he smashed a daisy cutter to Doc at third.

"Leggit! Leggit!" chanted the rooters again.

However, Doc's frozen rope across the infield retired this batter by a step too.

Two hands down.

FROZEN ROPE: *hard line drive or throw.*

HAND DOWN: *an out.* ONE HAND DOWN *meant "one out,"* TWO HANDS DOWN *meant "two outs,"* and THREE HANDS DOWN (or DEAD) *meant "three outs."*

The Travelin' Nine whipped the rock around the infield. Not only had they retired the first two Cincinnati strikers, but in the process they had also silenced the fans.

The third batter strode to the plate. All business, he crowded the dish and stared menacingly at Happy.

Ruby grinned knowingly.

Happy windmilled his arm and fired a fastball just below the striker's chin. The striker arched away and stumbled from the plate.

ROCK:
the baseball. Also called the "pill" (see page 44).

"That'll teach you!" Ruby cheered.

The striker inched back into the batter's box, and when he settled in, he stood a full boot's-length away from the dish.

Happy windmilled his arm and fired again. The batter closed his eyes and swung.

Crack!

"Oh, no!" Graham cried as the ball soared

He started jogging backward . . .

toward the deepest part of right garden.

"Easy, Grammy." Griffith placed a hand on his brother's shoulder. "Woody's got it."

And sure enough, Woody drifted back, gracefully lifted his glove, and caught the ball.

Three hands dead.

Woody picked the ball from the glove. He knelt down, placed his leather on the field, because both teams shared the same glove when they patrolled the outfield, and stood back up, raising the ball high over his head and whirling around on his toes like a ballerina. Then he started jogging *backward* toward the players' bench.

"There goes Woody!" Griffith announced.

Graham placed one hand on his brother's shoulder and one on his sister's. "Like Doc and the Professor always tell us, Woody loves baseball so much—"

"—he'll never turn his back on the game!" all three cheered together.

9

★

Barnstormers at Bat

"e're up," **Ruby** announced, biting her lower lip.

"C'mon, Crazy Feet!" Graham cheered the Travelin' Nine's leadoff hitter. "C'mon, Tales," he cheered their number-two hitter in the on-deck circle.

The two table setters at the top of the lineup went right to work, stroking consecutive singles to left field. Woody then followed with an ant killer to first that moved both Crazy Feet and Tales into scoring position. That set up Scribe to bring the runs home.

TABLE SETTERS:
Sometimes the first two batters in the lineup are called the "table setters." They "set the table" for all the other strikers in the batting order by getting on base.

ANT KILLER:
ground ball. Also called "grass clipper" (see page 68) or "daisy cutter" (see page 48).

And Scribe delivered! A deep double to right scored two tallies.

"Go, barnstormers!" Ruby shouted. She then turned to Griffith. "Daddy would've loved this."

"He sure would have." Griffith leaned into his sister. "Baseball like it oughta be!"

"Hot fun in the summertime!" Ruby added.

"I knew we'd win!" Graham saluted the Travelin' Nine. "I knew it!"

"Easy, Grammy," Griffith cautioned. "It's only the first inning. There's still a lot of baseball left to be played."

Ruby wiped her brow. It was hot, too hot to be standing so close to her brothers. So at the end of the first frame, with the Travelin' Nine ahead by two runs, Ruby stepped away. As she did, she pulled the baseball from her brothers and slid it into her side pocket.

"What are you doing?" Griffith asked. "Where are you going?"

"I'm not going anywhere," Ruby replied.

"Ruby, we have to stay together."

"We are together, Griffy, but we can't stand huddled like this the entire game. It's a hundred degrees in the shade!"

"But the Travelin' Nine are winning," Griffith said. "We shouldn't change a thing. You know better than that. You know how superstitious Daddy used to be when it came to baseball."

"Listen, Griff," Ruby said. "We're doing exactly what Daddy would've wanted."

"I'm not sure, Ruby."

"But I am. Trust me. This is together." She drew a circle in the air around them. "We may not be touching each other, but there's no doubt we're together."

10

★

From Out of Nowhere

**WHIP OF
THE WILLOW:**
swing of the bat.

n the second frame, the Cincinnati club clawed back, scoring on back-to-back triples, cutting the Travelin' Nine's lead in half. Then, with one mighty swing of the bat in the fourth, they added three more tallies when their center fielder launched one of Happy's curveballs deep into the trees beyond Crazy Feet in left.

What once was a two-run lead was now a two-run deficit, and the score was 4–2, Cincinnati.

What's more, that last whip of the willow awoke a sleeping giant. The Cincinnati crowd that had been silenced earlier was hailing barbs and cheering louder than ever.

Ruby and Griffith looked nervously at each other, and he whispered, "Get the ball out. I think we need to be holding the ball now."

Ruby pulled the baseball from her pocket and nudged Graham to get his attention away from the field.

"Everyone put your hand on the ball," she said. "The Travelin' Nine has taken a turn for the worse this frame, and I wonder . . ." Ruby didn't finish her thought, but both Graham and Griffith looked solemnly from her face to the ball they were each touching. Griffith felt himself hold his breath, Graham closed his eyes, and Ruby stood as still as she possibly could, willing the game to favor her team.

Each child felt the stillness surround them as Griffin softly repeated Uncle Owen's words, "We will be together. Always."

Then came a breeze. From out of nowhere.

Not a gust. Nor a gale. Just a gentle rush of air, barely enough to rustle leaves or bend blades of grass.

A presence. The first breath on a stifling day. One that caused a collective gasp from the fans.

Something had arrived.

"What's going on?" Ruby whispered.

"I'm not sure," Griffith whispered back.

11

★

A Looming Darkness

hat's happening, Griffy?" Graham cowered behind his brother.

"Doc doesn't . . . Doc doesn't know it's there!" Ruby stammered, still holding the ball in her now shaking hand although the boys had dropped their hands to turn and face the field.

Griffith stared at the object rising from the ground like a metal cornstalk behind Doc. He shaded his eyes as Doc sidestepped a few strides from the third bag and watched as Doc *felt* the shadow, a looming darkness. Suddenly, Doc whirled around and found himself inches from a hovering train signal, *growing* out of the ground. Doc gasped and lurched away just as the signal post's blade swung around, nearly taking off his head.

"How can that be?" Ruby's blue eyes bulged. She clutched the baseball as tightly as she could.

"Griffy, what's happening?" Graham asked again, grabbing hold of his brother's leg.

"I have no idea." Griffith could feel Graham trembling. "But it's because of the ball. We took out the ball, the breeze came, and then . . ." He peeked around to Ruby, who was now crouching behind his other side. "You can see the train signal, right?"

"Of course I can see it, Griff!" Ruby exclaimed. "Why do you think I'm hiding?"

"Well, they can't." Griffith motioned to the crowd and the opposing team. He pulled his still-quivering sister next to him.

Ruby covered her mouth with the hand that wasn't still grasping their father's baseball. Griffith was right. Doc was standing in foul territory, Bubbles had shifted over to the right side of the infield, and Crazy Feet was now positioned *behind* Scribe in center garden. But it was clear that not a Cincinnati soul—not the Swine, nor their supporters— could see the switching signal. Instead, they were focusing on the Travelin' Nine's most unusual defensive setup and wondering why their opponents were all staring at *nothing* by third sack.

Griffith ran a hand through his hair. Obviously the barnstormers could see the train post, but for some reason they didn't

"Doc doesn't know it's there!"

seem afraid. Sure, Doc had almost lost his head, and many of the others had shifted over and away, but for the most part the Travelin' Nine appeared only to be puzzled. If they had been frightened, Griffith realized, they would have all been racing from the field.

"How can that be?" Ruby asked again. "It's the ball—it has to be the ball, right?"

"How am I supposed to know?" Griffith wondered if Ruby could feel that he was shaking too.

"Griffy, what's it doing?" Graham inched out from behind his brother as the signal continued to rotate.

"I have no idea," Griffith replied. He glanced at the baseball in Ruby's hand, and for the briefest of moments, he thought he saw the ball *shiver*. He quickly looked back at the field. "I don't know anything."

12

★

How Could This Be?

hough Ruby tucked the ball back into her pocket, hoping to put a stop to the strange events on the field, it didn't work. The switching tower didn't remain by third bag for very long. As quickly as it appeared, it disappeared, *sinking* into the ground as fast as it rose.

But it didn't disappear for long. It kept popping out of the ground in different places—in left garden in front of Crazy Feet, near first sack alongside Professor Lance, and in short-center garden, behind Bubbles and Tales and in front of Scribe.

STINGER:
*a hard-hit ball,
usually a grounder
or a line drive.
Also known as a
"hammer" (see
page 103).*

PLATE (v.):
*to score a run,
or tally.*

One thing about the train post puzzled Griffith more than anything else. Wherever and whenever the signal emerged, its blade always swung, almost as if it were pointing at something.

As the game moved on, the Travelin' Nine struggled more and more, allowing another tally in the sixth. And watching the Cincinnati Swine bat in the seventh frame was like watching a merry-go-round. Every player leaped aboard and circled the bases. A stinger past a diving Tales plated one tally.

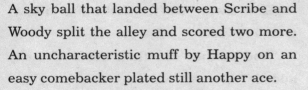

A sky ball that landed between Scribe and Woody split the alley and scored two more. An uncharacteristic muff by Happy on an easy comebacker plated still another ace.

Of course the fog didn't help matters either.

All through those middle innings a haunting gray mass had rolled in, consuming parts of the field and moving about from place to place much like the train signal. Yes, in the middle of a sweltering summer afternoon, a traveling fog had taken hold and taken over.

ALLEY:
either of two areas in the outfield, one between left garden and center garden and the other between right garden and center garden.

MUFF:
error.

ACE:
a run. Also known as a "tally" (see page 74).

"The Swine can't see the fog either," Graham said.

"And neither can their cranks," Ruby added.

Griffith realized his brother and sister were right. The Swine ran in and out of the fog, fielding sky balls and daisy cutters like it wasn't even there, while their fans still cheered on all the action taking place inside the low-hanging cloud.

Griffith's mind raced faster. None of this made *any* sense, if sense could possibly be

made of moving switching signals and fogs from nowhere. This was all just too much for him to process. He needed help. Could he trust his sister to keep the secret he'd been carrying around since their father's funeral? He decided he had no choice.

Griffith turned to Ruby. "Listen," he whispered, "there's something I need to tell you."

"I know."

Griffith sighed. Sometimes he hated how she could see right through him. "You can't say anything to Grammy."

"What is it?"

He took his sister by the arm and led her farther away from their brother. "It's something Uncle Owen said to me the night of the funeral."

"What did he say?"

"Something very strange." Griffith took a long breath. "He said, 'Things will speak to you. In different ways.'"

"So? What does that mean?" Ruby asked.

FOUR-BAGGER:
home run.

SCREAMER:
a hard-hit fly ball.

"That's what I've been trying to figure out." Griffith spoke to the field.

At long last the disastrous top half of the seventh frame ended, bringing the score to 10-2, Cincinnati Swine.

Fortunately the Travelin' Nine did manage to get a run back in their half of the seventh. Professor Lance connected for a four-bagger, a screamer past the train signal and through the invisible fog in right.

All the offense the barnstormers could muster

But that was all the offense the barn-stormers could muster.

"Do something!" Graham swatted his brother.

"What do you want me to do?"

"I don't know. Something." Graham lowered his chin and scrunched his face into a knot. "You're the oldest. You're supposed to be the smartest."

"I wonder," Ruby said cautiously, "if we should get the ball out again?"

Griffith shook his head no and thought for a moment. "Wait here. I'll be right back."

"Where are you going?" Ruby called.

Griffith was off without an answer. He stepped over, around, and through the root-ers until he stood among them, directly behind home plate in the space in front of the sign used for posting the tallies and innings. Then he slid down even closer, until he stood right behind the players' bench. Once there, he could see and hear everything.

He watched Guy returning her lumber to the spot beside the bench that served as the on-deck area. And he saw an exhausted Happy seated on the turf behind first sack, wilting in the heat. Then he looked at the other players on the bench—Scribe, Bubbles, Doc, and Woody—each looking

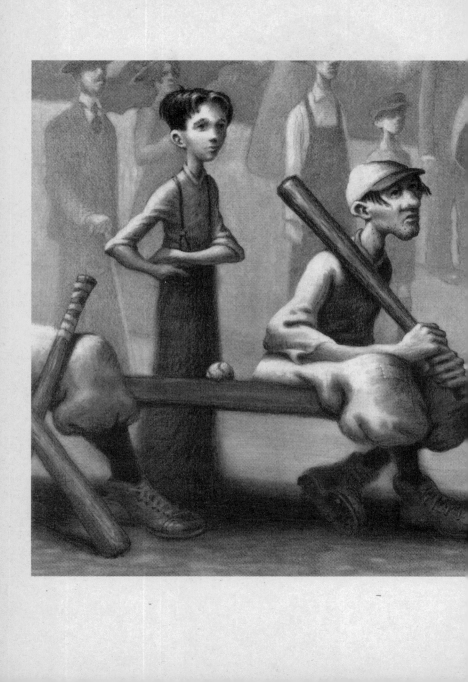

"It's just not possible."

more perplexed than the next.

"How could these things be happening?" Tales asked his teammates as they readied to take their positions to start the eighth frame. "It's just not possible."

"Anything's possible," Professor Lance corrected him. "We learned that back in Cuba."

"I reckon I don' know, Professor." Woody pointed to the field. "These things only happened when Guy was wit' us, and since he ain't here, I just don' git it."

Griffith blew out a small, frustrated puff of air. Indeed, the Travelin' Nine were as confused as he was.

What was he missing?

13

★

Fogs and Trains

huff! Chuff!
Griffith was jolted back to the pres-
ent. *Chuff! Chuff!* The low, rhythmic chugging
of the engine, the hiss of safety valves, and
even the call of a steam whistle—a symphony
of sounds now coming from *inside* the fog.

Chuff! Chuff!

Griffith raced up, around, and back
through the crowd to Ruby and Graham.
Charging back to his brother and sister, he
saw that not a single person in the crowd
spun their head or covered their ears. The

cranks couldn't hear the unmistakable sound of an approaching train!

"What's happening now?" Graham asked as Griffith sped over.

Griffith huddled his brother and sister in close but offered no answer.

Ruby's eyes remained fixed on the field. All of a sudden the fog began to lift like a curtain at the start of a show, and a line of railroad tracks now cut a diagonal straight across the pitch. It began in foul territory behind third sack and disappeared into the thick forest beyond right garden.

PITCH:
playing field.

All of the Travelin' Nine stopped and stared, mouths agape, mesmerized.

"The game goes on!" the umpire cried, gesturing to the Travelin' Nine, who to him were spellbound by nothing. He pointed at Happy to continue pitching.

Ruby could hardly stand to watch, because the moment Happy stepped to the hill, the sounds began again. Sapped of all his energy and sagging in the heat, he threw a pitch that *floated* over the plate. And as the ball approached the striker, a mammoth locomotive stormed down the tracks!

The Travelin' Nine leaped out of the way as if they were scrambling for their lives. Woody raced away from the train as the ball soared over his head into deep right garden. It was only because Woody was so masterful in the outfield—and so fleet of foot in the face of the train bearing down upon him—that he managed in a leaping spin to snag the ball off the ground, firing it to second, and holding the runner to a double. But the Cincinnati ballists and cranks didn't react at all. They couldn't see the roaring train engine either!

When Happy stepped back on the hill, the fog suddenly reappeared—this time in right garden. Then as quickly as it had appeared, it once again disappeared, this time leaving

The mammoth locomotive

behind a trail of tracks across the entire outer garden.

Happy threw his next pitch (which barely even reached the dish), and as the ball approached the striker, the mammoth locomotive once again tore down the tracks. The Travelin' Nine scrambled one more time.

That's how it went while the Travelin' Nine were on the field for both the eighth and the ninth innings. Each time Happy windmilled his arm and rocked into his windup, he faced a conspiracy of noises. The whistles and chuffs grew louder and faster, as if his arm were cranking up the sounds into the deafening and intimidating roar. And then, each time the ball left his hand, the enormous train engine roared through the field.

But to Ruby, one thing about the fog and ghost train puzzled her more than anything else—the way it moved about the field and traveled in different directions.

The Cincinnati Swine had a grand time of it . . . even though all they could see was the dumbfounded reactions of the Travelin' Nine.

A hammer flew past a diving Doc—only Doc was diving from the dust and smoke rather than for the ball. A stunner soared past a leaping Tales—only Tales was leaping from the pebbles and dirt rather than for the ball.

"Something's wrong," Griffith whispered.

"What do you mean?" said Ruby.

"I don't know," Griffith replied, "but I know we shouldn't be losing like this."

Griffith gestured to Ruby to take the ball out of her pocket again. He thought back to the train signals that had appeared earlier in the game. The way they pointed in different directions puzzled him the most.

"You're right," Ruby agreed. "I don't think we should be losing like this either."

They all reached out and gripped the ball

HAMMER:
a hard-hit ball.
Also known
as a "stinger"
(see page 86).

STUNNER:
a ball that is hit
hard, usually on
the ground.

even tighter than before. Maybe the Travelin' Nine shouldn't be leaping out of the way. Maybe they should be staying put. It almost seemed like the fog and the train were trying to show them something. She just couldn't figure out what.

"I don't know what to do," Griffith and Ruby said at the exact same moment.

"Do you two know *anything*?" Graham asked.

They did. In fact, Griffith, Ruby, and Graham were all certain of one thing: The Travelin' Nine were moments away from losing the game.

14

★

Huzzah!

uzzah!" **Happy tipped**
his cap to the host team
and waved it to the
remaining rooters. While Happy still wasn't
his usual energetic self, he looked far better than he had on the mound those last
innings.

"On behalf of the Travelin' Nine," he
proclaimed, "I would like to say thank you
kindly for a wonderful match, a glorious day,
and most of all, your generous hospitality."

Ruby sat atop second sack with her open
journal resting in her lap. For the moment,

"HUZZAH!":
*common cheer to
show appreciation
for a team's
efforts.*

she only had time to jot down some brief notes about the afternoon—the things she saw and thought she saw, as well as the constant questions that had been whirling around in her head. Later, back at the inn or on their way to Louisville, when she had more time, Ruby would write more. She was now sure that their baseball could have given the Travelin' Nine the chance to win the game. She wasn't sure how or why, just that it could have if only they had understood more about how to use the strange occurrences on the field. *Things will speak to you. In different ways.* The train signal, the fog, the running train tracks, and the roaring trains had all been speaking to them. What had they been saying, though?

Ruby thought back to the first time the train had appeared. Woody had managed to snag the ball on a bounce and hold the runner on second. But the ball had soared too far for him to catch, even if he hadn't been distracted

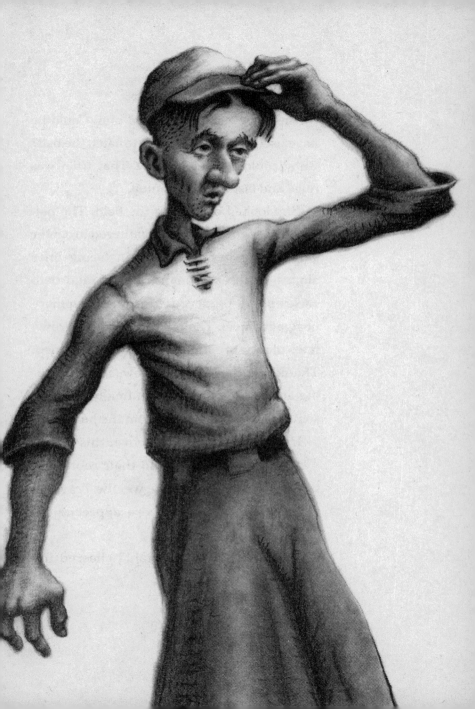

by the train barreling toward him. Could he have used the tracks or train to catch the ball? Ruby couldn't imagine how. That train was huge and fast and frightening. . . .

She looked out across the field. The ballists from both squads had gathered in center garden and were standing in facing lines alongside an assortment of foods and delicacies set to be devoured at the customary postgame meal. Though the hour had grown late, plenty of summer daylight remained. Thankfully, the longer shadows now stretching across the outer garden finally afforded some long-awaited relief from the heat.

Happy placed his cap over his heart. "To this fine ball club and their rooters in this fair city of Cincinnati, we, the Travelin' Nine, say to you in sincere appreciation, hip . . . hip . . . huzzah!"

"Hip . . . hip . . . huzzah!" cheered the barnstormers.

A pig roast with all the fixin's

"Hip . . . hip . . . huzzah!" cheered the Cincinnati Swine. They tossed their caps to the sky.

The traditional feast commenced. And since they were in Porkopolis, the feast was a pig roast with all the fixin's.

Ruby closed up her journal and joined Graham and Griffith at the festivities.

But Griffith was hardly in a festive frame of mind. He could not digest the afternoon's defeat. Something didn't feel right. He still believed he should have been able to do something. He just didn't know what.

He looked out at the Travelin' Nine. To them, this first loss was merely a minor setback. They had survived the horrors of war, and a lone loss on a baseball field was hardly a reason to feel dejected or downtrodden. The Travelin' Nine were as upbeat as ever.

"Hunky play out there," Tales told the Cincinnati second baseman. "Wish I'd been

HUNKY:
splendid, as in "hunky play."

110

able to swing the timber like you did today."

"That there was some mighty square work in the field," Doc said to the hometown center fielder. "Let me tell you, the way you strike, you could play for the Red Stockings!"

The Swine's power-hitting center scout tipped his cap and then turned to Guy. "I must say, you're quite the backstop. I've been around this game for some years now, and I haven't seen many play behind with the ginger you do. What'd you say your name was?"

"Guy." She swallowed. "They call me Guy."

When Graham giggled, Griffith swatted him instantly.

"Guy's the best catcher in all the land," Ruby chimed in. "Soon every ballist from New York to New Orleans will play behind the dish like sh—like him. Just you watch."

Guy winked at her daughter.

Ruby was about to say more, but Bubbles

CENTER SCOUT: *center fielder.*

BEHIND: *catcher. Also called "backstop" (see page 41).*

GINGER: *hustle and enthusiasm.*

had already begun to tell his tales from growing up in the Queen City of the West. Unfortunately for him, as Ruby noted when she scanned the faces of the Cincinnati Swine, no one seemed particularly interested.

"As I'm sure you know, my fellow Cincinnatians, the 1869 Red Stockings team was one of a kind, still the only team ever to go undefeated for an entire season. My uncle Theodore played for that nine."

"He did?" said one of the players. "Never heard of no Theodore on the '69 Stockings."

"Well . . . um . . . he should have. He should
have been playing right alongside Harry
Wright, Fred Waterman, and all the other
greats."

"Then why didn't he, Babbles? I mean, er,
Bubbles," the same Cincinnati player asked.
There were some muffled snickers from the
other players.

"Not only was Uncle Theodore quite the
ballist, but he was also quite the inventor.
Once those boys over at Procter & Gamble
caught wind of what Uncle Theodore could

do, they snatched him up. He went to work for them instead."

"Oh, Bubbles." Ruby plopped down beside him and nudged him teasingly. "You do love to tell a story."

"That's the truth." Bubbles pointed at the other players. "You could ask him yourself. These days he's up in Dayton with cousins Orville and Wilbur. They're building some flying contraption or something."

As afternoon faded into evening, the foes-turned-friends drank and dined, built bonds, and swapped stories. Of course, all the Cincinnati players sat entranced by the barn-stormers' tales from the Spanish-American War, hanging on to every last word of the firsthand accounts of the Rough Riders and San Juan Hill.

"War heroes with stories from the battle-field are a huge attraction," the Cincinnati hurler said. "Once word spreads about how well you play, everyone's going to want to see you in action."

"That's what we're all hoping will happen," Professor Lance replied.

The Cincinnati backstop chuckled. "And I say the way y'all carry on out there, reckon it makes for a most entertainin' afternoon, for players and rooters alike, if you don't mind me sayin'."

"I have to admit," the hurler added, "winning sure is sweeter when beating such a zany opponent."

"Now if you don't mind me askin'," the Cincinnati catcher spoke up again, "why do y'all carry on like that? Starin' off in diff'rent directions, actin' like you be seein' things on the field. If I didn't know better, I reckon you'd seen ghosts!"

The Travelin' Nine suddenly got quiet.

Professor Lance adjusted the cord of

the patch that covered his left eye. Tales flicked the beads of sweat from the tips of his twitching bushy mustache. Bubbles scratched his left ear. Doc beat his bowlegs with his hands. Even Scribe tucked his quill behind his right ear and looked up from his leather-bound journal, in which he had been jotting memories of the day.

Griffith, Ruby, and Graham could *taste* the unease and uncertainty among the former soldiers.

"Well, that's all part of the plan," Professor Lance finally answered. "We're hoping it brings the fans to the field."

15

★

Something Else . . .

ike he had before the start of the game, Griffith sat alone on the grassy knoll underneath the great oak beyond right garden. He peered down at the Travelin' Nine now gathered around the players' bench. The hour was growing late, so Professor Lance and Doc had called the team together.

But Griffith hadn't joined them. He wanted to be alone because he still couldn't get thoughts of that train signal out of his head. He kept thinking about how it popped up in all different places and how the arm kept pointing in different directions. Was that where the Travelin' Nine were supposed to play? Was that where they were supposed to hit? Was that how the switching signal was *speaking* to him?

Ruby hadn't joined the team meeting either. Like Griffith, she wanted to be alone because she couldn't get the thoughts of the train tracks and the racing locomotive out of her head. She sat down on the field again (this time atop third sack), removed the baseball from her pocket, and placed it next to her journal as she wrote:

Tracks: Straight across infield
Left garden foul line to outer-
right garden
Pitcher's line to first sack
Train: Across infield, first-base
bag to third-base bag

Across outer garden, left to right
First bag to third bag

Ruby chewed on her pen. The tracks would appear in different places and the locomotive would speed through in different directions. She still felt certain they were showing her a way to something. Surely the train tracks and the locomotive were *speaking* to her.

She closed up her journal and, with the ball still in her hand, she walked up the grassy knoll to Griffith.

"What are you doing up here?" she asked.

"Thinking."

"About what?"

Griffith patted the ground beside him. "I need to tell you something else, Ruby."

"What is it?" She sat down next to her brother and handed him the baseball.

"Uncle Owen said something else to me." He faced his sister.

"You haven't told me everything?"

"Not everything."

"So there's more?"

Griffith placed the ball back in her hand. "Ruby, Uncle Owen said there's a great danger."

Ruby felt the hairs on her arms tingle. "What type of danger?"

"I'm not sure." Griffith paused and felt himself frown. "But he said it was an unspeakable kind. He said . . ."

Just then Graham charged up the hill from the field. "Hey! What are you two doing?"

"Talking about you," Griffith teased.

"You were?"

"We sure were, Grammy," Ruby said. She slipped the ball back into her pocket and stood up. "We were saying how it's really important that all three of us work together to try to help the Travelin' Nine." She looked at her older brother.

"We have to work as a team."

"Ruby's right." Griffith stood up too. "When it comes to helping the Travelin' Nine, we can't do things separately. We have to work as a team."

"Just like Uncle Owen said," Graham chimed in. "We have to be together. Always."

"And I know something we can do together," Ruby said, placing a hand on each brother's shoulder. "Let's go hear what the Travelin' Nine have to say."

16

★

Team Meeting

riffith, Ruby, and Graham headed down the grassy knoll toward the players' bench, where the Travelin' Nine had gathered.

"Gentlemen." Professor Lance stood before the group. "As you know, we leave the field today with many, many questions."

"We all saw what happened out there," Doc added. "My friends, we all understand there must be a reason."

The Professor, Doc, and all the others were so focused on the business at hand that

they didn't even notice that the three Paynes had joined them. They still didn't notice even when Ruby sat down on the end of the bench.

"I reckon it doesn't make much sense," said Woody. "Durin' the war, when these things occurred, it was 'cause of Guy. But now, how can it be happenin' wit'out him?"

"Guy always said the things happened because of us." Bubbles scratched the remains of his left ear.

"That's true," Tales replied. "But that doesn't explain how we could see the

switching signal, the fog, and the train, but
all the town folks couldn't."

"And what was a switchin' signal, a fog,
and a train doin' here in the first place?"
Woody asked.

"My friends." Doc silenced his teammates with his hands. "These questions need
answers, but I don't have those answers.
Neither do the Professor, nor Scribe, nor any
of us. But I firmly believe we need answers
before our next game in Louisville. That's
only five days from now."

"Lindy, I couldn't agree more"—Professor

Lance cleared his throat—"but I believe a matter of even greater importance must first be addressed." He rubbed the patch that covered his left eye. "Under no circumstances can we afford to let what happened here in Cincinnati happen anywhere else. We cannot walk away from *any* future matches having earned no money. We must raise that ten thousand dollars. The consequences, as you know . . . the consequences are far too dire."

Griffith wasn't certain if Ruby and Graham understood what the barnstormers were saying, but he did. The match between the Cincinnati Swine and the Travelin' Nine had been winner take all. The squad that won the game won all the ticket money, while the losing team received none of the gate receipts. It was the only way the Cincinnati ballists would agree to play.

The Cincinnati Swine earned $718. The Travelin' Nine earned nothing.

Suddenly Griffith realized he had been staring, staring at the pocket where Ruby kept their baseball. He wondered how long he had been looking at it. Then, for a moment, he thought he saw her pocket *tremble*.

17

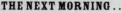

Off to Louisville

THE NEXT MORNING...

Graham tugged at his sister. "Let's go, Ruby."

"Hold on, Grammy." She tugged back.

"I don't want to miss the boat!" Graham pointed toward the river.

From the moment he had learned they would be traveling by steamboat to Louisville, Graham had hardly been able to control his excitement. Down the hill and around the bend, *his* steamboat awaited. Over the chimneys he could see the smoke from the tall stacks billowing into the cloudless sky. He could even make out the sound of the paddle-wheels churning the waters by the wharf.

"Grammy, we're not leaving here until Woody and Griff get back from the post office," Ruby said.

"Don't worry, son," Happy added. "That steamer won't leave the dock without you."

That was all Graham needed to hear. When it came to matters of transportation and travel, Happy knew better than anyone. Happy was a train man; he had spent most of his life riding the rails. And he had used the connections he had made from years of rail time to map out and arrange for the Travelin' Nine's trip to Cincinnati.

But for a while last night even Graham could sense that an anxious uncertainty was hanging over the Travelin' Nine. Since they hadn't earned a single cent in Cincinnati, how would they possibly afford the trip to Louisville?

His steamboat awaited.

It wasn't until late into the evening that Happy had recovered enough and found the energy to begin making the arrangements. However, by that hour, the only train heading to Louisville was an express one. Even with all of Happy's connections, the Travelin' Nine couldn't afford it, and the next local train would not get them to Louisville in time to properly promote and play the match.

Yet somehow Happy found a way to work some of his old railroad magic. Well, not exactly railroad. If the barnstormers were to have any hope of reaching Louisville in time, they would have to travel by steamboat.

Graham had never been on a steamboat because in 1899 steamboat travel wasn't nearly what it used to be; floating palaces had been replaced by railroads. But suddenly, the steamboat had become necessary and relevant all over again.

"Here they come!" Graham pointed. He raced up the block to Griffith and Woody. "Was there a letter from Uncle Owen?"

Griffith forced a smile. "There sure was."

"Yes!" Graham jumped. "What did it say?"

"Hold on there," Griffith replied as they walked toward their mother. "We have a steamer to catch. I'll tell you when we're all aboard."

More than anything that morning, Griffith had wanted to hear from Uncle Owen. He had hoped his letter would provide some answers.

But instead of answers, he had gotten something else. He turned to Ruby.

"What is it?" Ruby asked.

"Nothing." On the boat, he would show her the letter and the three most disturbing words he had ever seen on a page: "Beware the Chancellor."

This was the unspeakable danger. And

this greedy, relentless man—this monstrous man—was a greater threat than any Griffith might have dreamed.

"Can I say something?" Ruby gave Griffith a quick, knowing glance and then halted, pulling both her brothers in close. "I'm thinking of something Daddy always told us."

"What's that?" Graham asked.

"Daddy used to say that in life we often can't control what happens to us, but what we can control is—"

"—how we deal with it." The three Paynes finished the sentence.

As she watched her three children, Elizabeth's eyes began to fill.

"What's the matter, Mom?" Graham asked. "Are you crying?"

Elizabeth smiled. She tousled her youngest son's hair. "Oh, I'm fine. Believe it or not, in spite of everything, I'm happy. I have the three of you." She hugged her children as tightly as she could.

As she did, Ruby slowly and carefully lifted the baseball from her pocket. She held it in such a way that only Griffith could

see it. Griffith didn't say a word. Instead, he reached over and touched the baseball. He nodded to his sister, and Ruby nodded back.

When she did, Griffith knew he had done the right thing in telling Ruby what Uncle Owen had said.

But Griffith was also beginning to recall something else, a distant memory or a dream that the letter had triggered. He had this budding feeling that Graham was somehow inexplicably tied to this whole thing. All of it. The money, the events on the field, the unspeakable danger. Somehow this was all about protecting Graham. He just had to figure out why.

"Are we ready?" Elizabeth asked.

"I'm ready," Graham replied.

"I second that." Ruby carefully slipped the baseball back into her pocket.

"Then let's go to Louisville," finished Griffith.

★

See what's on deck!

Read a chapter from the Travelin' Nine's

next game,

HORSIN' AROUND,

AVAILABLE NOW!

★

The Game Begins

As if the umpire's call was her cue,
Ruby removed the baseball from her side
pocket and placed it in Griffith's open hand.
Then she hurried over to Graham, still standing by the players' bench, and walked him
down the left field line to Griffith.

It was time.

They stood among the cranks, but none in
the crowd were paying attention to them. All
eyes were fixed on the field.

Griffith held the baseball out to his
brother and sister, and just like they had

before the game in Cincinnati, all three joined hands on it.

"Here we go," Ruby said.

"Start us off!" Griffith called as Crazy Feet stepped to the plate.

Crazy Feet was the ideal leadoff batter. Not only could he run like the wind, but he could hit to all fields, work out a walk, and even provide some thunder at the top of the lineup.

THUNDER: *power.* *Also called "pop"*

"C'mon, Crazy Feet!" Graham cheered nervously.

Rube Waddell's first pitch was a fastball, but a fastball unlike any they had ever seen. The ball moved! As it blazed a path toward the plate, it fluttered from side to side.

Crazy Feet tried to check his confused swing, but he couldn't, popping up meekly to the pitcher.

The moment the ball landed in the

Louisville Lightning's leather, he leaped off the mound and clicked his heels. He danced in circles as all the cranks—especially those crammed into Rube's Rooters' Row—hooted and hollered.

One hand down.

"C'mon, Tales!" Ruby cheered as the Travelin' Nine's second sack man stepped to the plate.

Graham lifted his hand off the baseball and stepped in front of his brother and sister.

"Where are you going?" Griffith asked.

"I want to get a better view," Graham answered.

"We all should have a hand on the baseball," Ruby said.

"That didn't help Crazy Feet." Graham gestured to the Travelin' Nine's left scout.

At the dish, Tales dug in. He flapped his elbow four times, but fared no better. He

SECOND SACK MAN: *second baseman. The first baseman was often called the "first sack man" and the third baseman was often called the "third sack man."*

grounded out with a hit that would have barely bruised a bug.

Two hands down.

"They're not looking too good." Graham peered up at his brother and sister.

Griffith nodded. He looked at the baseball in his hands and then back at his brother. Had Graham let go of the ball too soon? Ruby was right; they all should hold on to the ball longer. Perhaps that was the reason things weren't going well for the Travelin' Nine.

"It's only the top of the first," Ruby replied. "The Rough Riders aren't even loose yet. They're still warming up."

"I hope you're right." Graham looked to the diamond again. "C'mon, Woody!" he cheered as the barnstormers' right scout stepped to the line.

Not only did Woody have a reliable glove and the strongest outfield arm on

STEP TO THE LINE
(V.): *to prepare to hit.*

the squad, but he was also a specialist with the lumber. All of the Travelin' Nine knew Woody was the best all-around striker on the team.

But against the Louisville Lightning, Woody fared even worse than Crazy Feet and Tales (if that was possible).

Fastball. Strike one.

Fastball. Strike two.

Fastball. Strike three!

Three hands dead. In the blink of an eye, the inning was over.

In the bottom of the first, the Louisville Summer Sluggers struck fast and frequently. By the end of the opening frame, the barnstormers already trailed by three tallies.

As Scribe stepped to the dish to start the second, Griffith pulled Graham closer.

"Stand back over here with us," he said

to his younger brother. "Let's all hold the ball again. Maybe that will help turn things around."

But even with all three Paynes touching their baseball, the Travelin' Nine's fortunes didn't exactly improve in that second frame.

Neither Griffith nor his brother or sister spoke a sentence or moved a muscle when Scribe grounded to first, Professor Lance popped to third, and Doc Linden stuck out. And neither Griffith nor his brother or sister spoke a sentence or moved a muscle when the Louisville Nine tacked on two more tallies to the three they had recorded in the first.

"They're getting destroyed!" Graham exclaimed.

"It's only been two innings," Ruby said, tucking the ball back into her pocket.

"There's plenty of baseball left to be played," Griffith added.

But as much as Griffith wanted to believe that, he couldn't help but share some of his brother's doubts.

Step u
ReadS
details a
Payne,

ReadSluggers.com is designed for true Sluggers' fans! You can check out excerpts from all the books, read exclusive interviews with both authors and get the latest updates.

Get on the ball!
Join Team Sluggers today!